THIS WHERE'S WALLY? BOOK BELONGS TO:

_____

_____

HEY, WALLY FANS! FIVE INTREPID TRAVELLERS
ARE LOST IN EVERY SCENE! CAN YOU FIND THEM?

| ODLAW | WIZARD WHITEBEARD | WENDA | WOOF | WALLY |

AND IN EVERY SCENE, THE TRAVELLERS
HAVE EACH LOST SOMETHING PRECIOUS!
CAN YOU FIND THEM TOO?

WALLY'S KEY ⌐ WOOF'S BONE ⌐ WENDA'S CAMERA

WIZARD WHITEBEARD'S SCROLL ⌐ ODLAW'S BINOCULARS

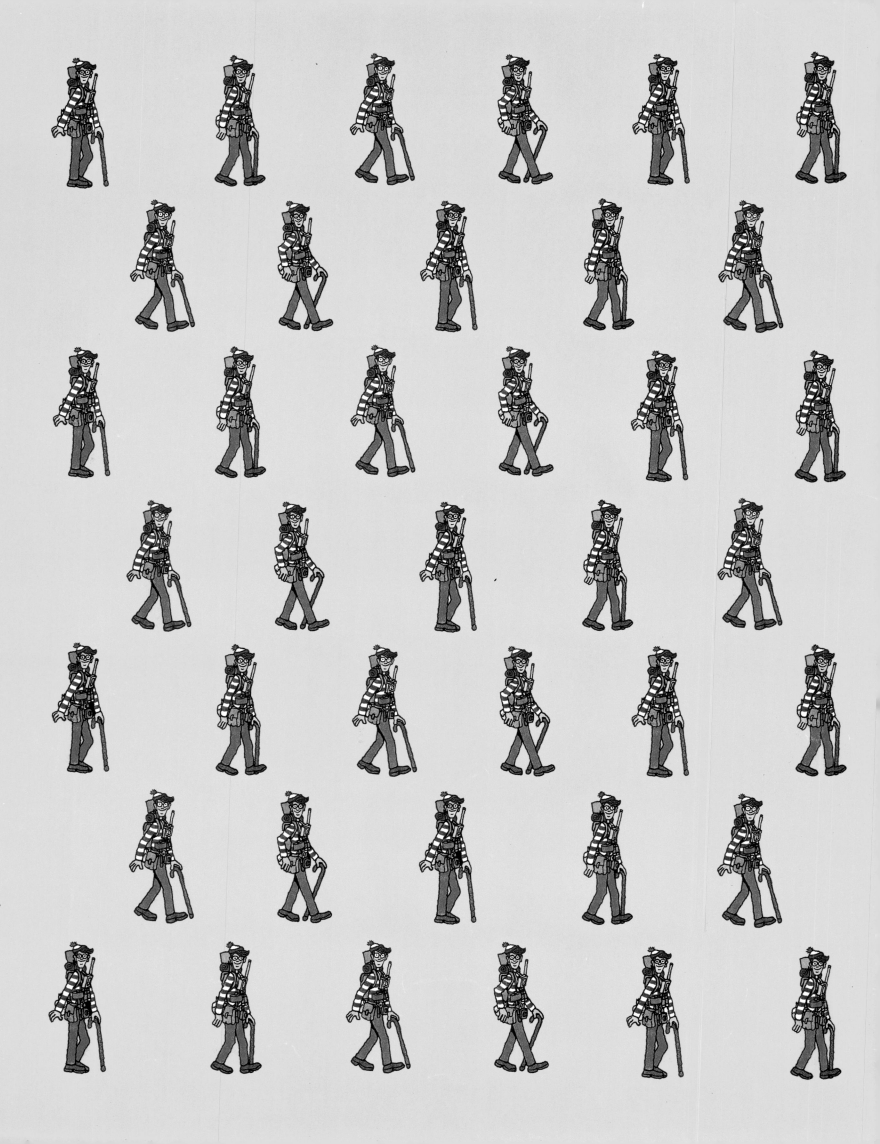

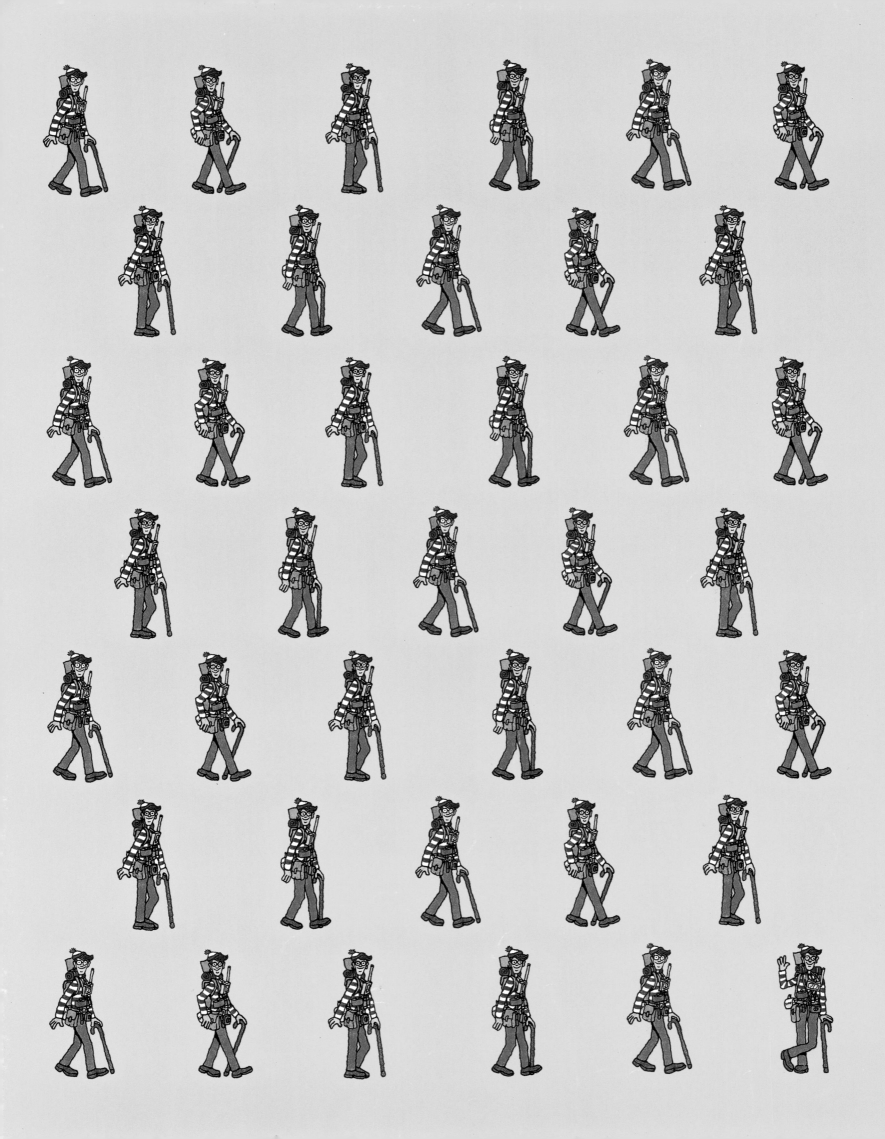

For Wally

First published 1987 by Walker Books Ltd
87 Vauxhall Walk, London SE11 5HJ

This edition published 2017

2 4 6 8 10 9 7 5 3 1

© 1987 – 2017 Martin Handford

The right of Martin Handford to be identified as author/illustrator
of this work has been asserted by him in accordance with the
Copyright, Designs and Patents Act 1988.

This book has been typeset in Wallyfont and Optima.

Printed in China

British Library Cataloguing in Publication Data:
a catalogue record for this book
is available from the British Library.

ISBN 978-1-4063-7569-5

www.walker.co.uk

MARTIN HANDFORD

WALKER BOOKS
AND SUBSIDIARIES
LONDON · BOSTON · SYDNEY · AUCKLAND

HI FRIENDS!

MY NAME IS WALLY. I'M JUST SETTING OFF ON A WORLDWIDE HIKE. YOU CAN COME TOO. ALL YOU HAVE TO DO IS FIND ME.

I'VE GOT ALL I NEED – WALKING STICK, KETTLE, MALLET, CUP, RUCKSACK, SLEEPING BAG, BINOCULARS, CAMERA, SNORKEL, BELT, BAG AND SHOVEL.

I'M NOT TRAVELLING ON MY OWN. WHEREVER I GO, THERE ARE LOTS OF OTHER CHARACTERS FOR YOU TO SPOT. FIRST FIND WOOF (BUT ALL YOU CAN SEE IS HIS TAIL), WENDA, WIZARD WHITEBEARD AND ODLAW. THEN FIND 25 WALLY-WATCHERS SOMEWHERE, EACH OF WHOM APPEARS ONLY ONCE ON MY TRAVELS. CAN YOU FIND ONE OTHER CHARACTER WHO APPEARS IN EVERY SCENE? ALSO IN EVERY SCENE, CAN YOU SPOT MY KEY, WOOF'S BONE, WENDA'S CAMERA, WIZARD WHITEBEARD'S SCROLL, AND ODLAW'S BINOCULARS?

WOW! WHAT A SEARCH!

Wally

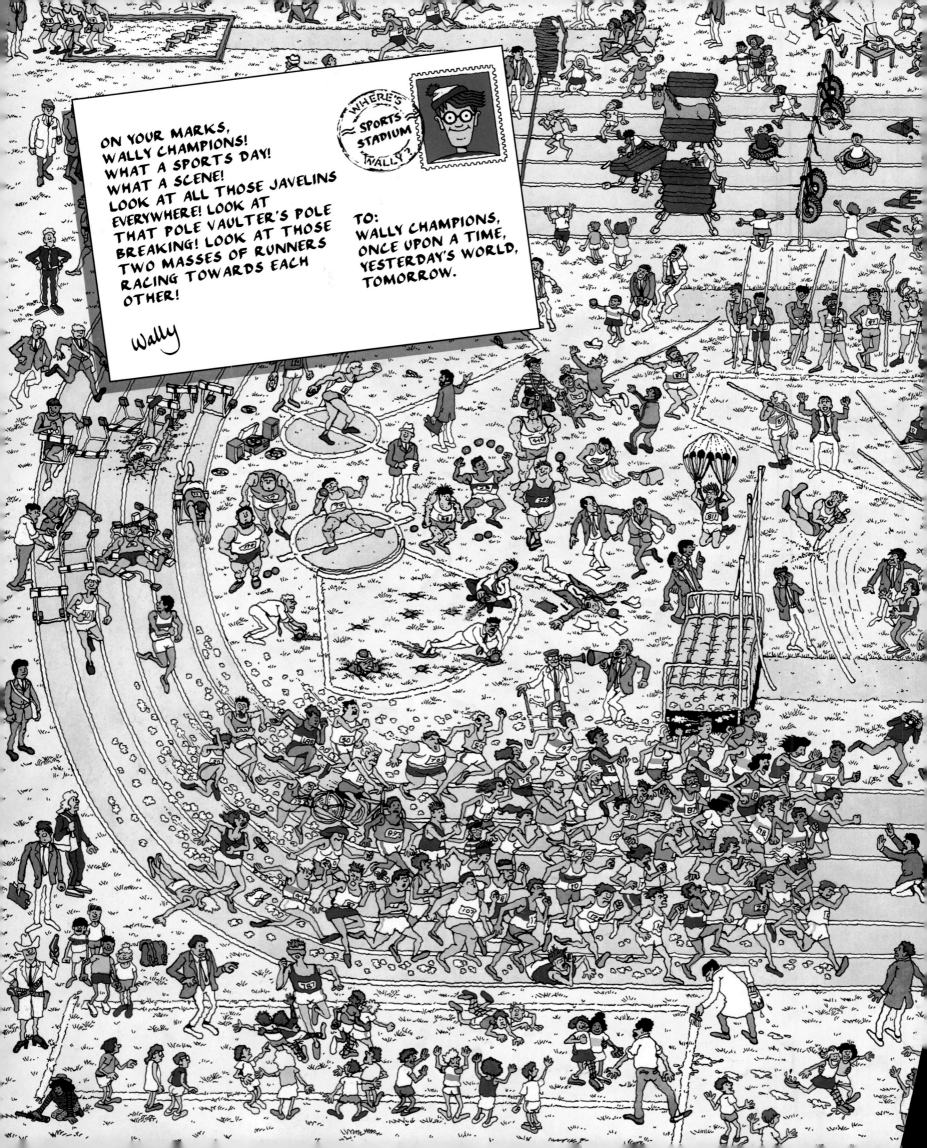

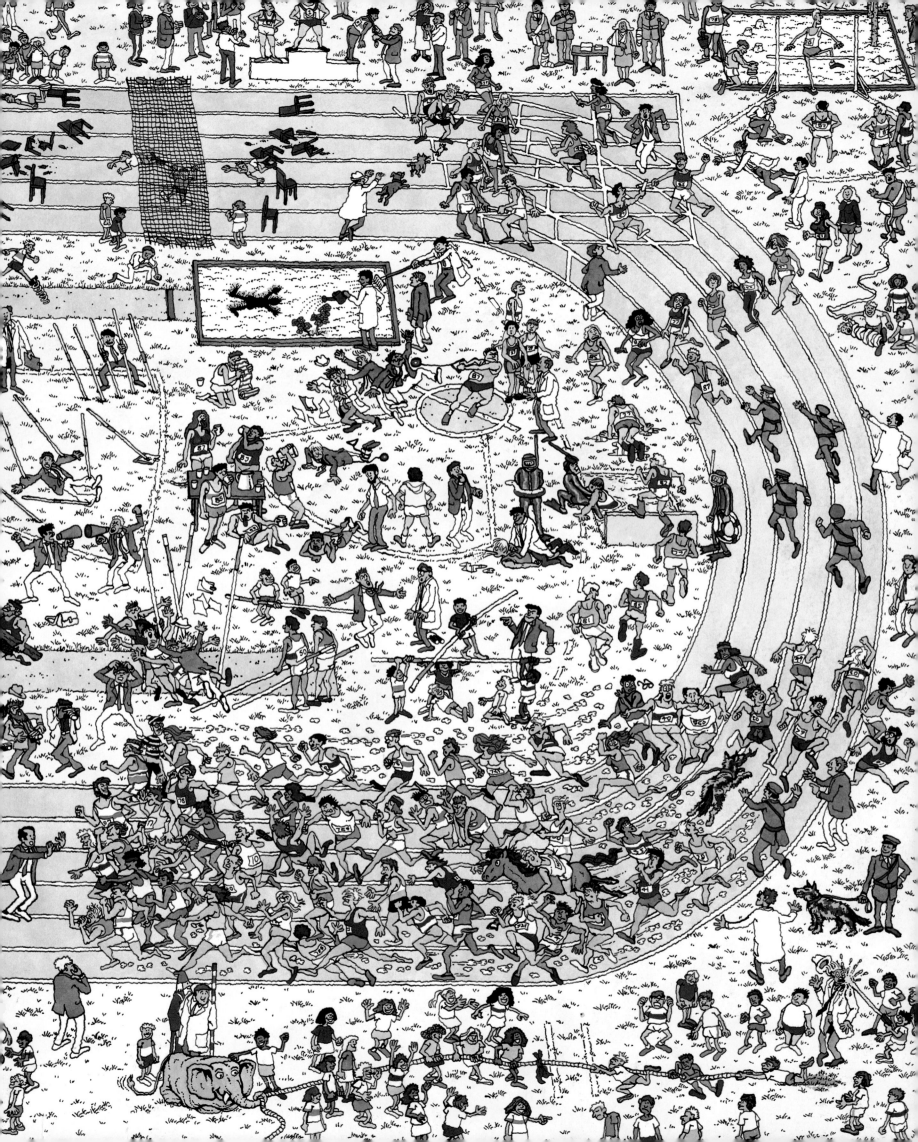

THE GREAT WHERE'S WALLY? CHECKLIST
Hundreds more things for Wally-watchers to watch out for!

IN TOWN
- A dog on a roof
- A man on a fountain
- A man about to trip over a dog's lead
- A car crash
- A keen barber
- People in a street, watching television
- A puncture caused by an arrow
- A tearful tune
- A boy attacked by a plant
- A sandwich
- A waiter who isn't concentrating
- Two firemen waving at each other
- A face on a wall
- A man coming out of a man hole
- A man feeding birds

SKI SLOPES
- A man reading on a roof
- A flying skier
- A runaway skier
- A backward skier
- A portrait in snow
- An illegal fisherman
- Five people wearing stripy scarves
- Snow about to fall on two laughing men
- Three skiers who have hit trees
- An Alpine horn
- Two broken flagpoles
- A flag collector
- Four people in yellow-hooded tops
- A skier up a tree
- A water skier on snow
- A Yeti
- Two skiing reindeer
- A roof jumper
- Someone crashing through five skiers

THE RAILWAY STATION
- Four shovels and five spades
- A trolley carrying five suitcases
- People being knocked over by a door
- A man about to step on a ball
- Three different times at the same time
- A wheelbarrow pram
- A face on a train
- Five people reading one newspaper
- A show-off with a suitcase
- Someone tripping over a dog
- Two men with red-and-white-striped ties
- A smoking train
- A squeeze on a bench
- A dog tearing a man's trousers
- A man sitting on a suitcase
- Twenty cows
- Someone struggling to lift a suitcase
- Two suitcases spilling their contents
- A broken weighing machine

ON THE BEACH
- A dog and its owners wearing sunglasses
- A man who is overdressed
- A muscular medallion man
- A water skier
- A stripy photographer
- A punctured lilo
- A donkey who likes ice cream
- A man being squashed
- A punctured beach ball
- A human pyramid
- Three people reading newspapers
- A cowboy
- A human donkey
- A radio
- A cross-looking human stepping-stone
- A red lilo
- Age and beauty
- Two red-and-yellow umbrellas
- Two men with vests, one without
- A show-off with sandcastles
- Someone wearing braces
- A cream coloured dog
- Three protruding tongues
- Two oddly fitting hats
- Five sprinters
- A towel with a hole in it
- A punctured hovercraft
- A boy who's not allowed any ice cream
- Two caps with extra-long peaks

CAMP SITE
- A bull in a hedge
- Bull horns
- A shark in a canal
- A bull seeing red
- A careless kick
- Tea in a lap
- A low bridge
- A person knocked over by a mallet
- A man surprised undressing
- A bicycle tyre about to be punctured
- Six dogs
- A scarecrow that doesn't work
- A wigwam
- Large biceps
- Three campers with very long beards
- A collapsed tent
- A smoking barbecue
- A fisherman catching old boots
- A winning penny-farthing
- A boy scout making fire
- A roller hiker
- A man blowing up a dinghy
- Thirsty walkers
- Runners on the road
- A bull chasing two people
- A camper's butler

AIRPORT
- A flying saucer
- A boy sitting with the revolving luggage
- A leaking fuel pipe
- Flight controllers playing badminton
- A rocket
- A tower on top of the control tower
- Three watch smugglers
- An airport worker resting on a plane
- A forklift truck
- A wind-sock
- Someone with a bucket and spade
- Six air hostesses in light blue uniforms
- A plane with giant tail wings
- A fire engine and ten firemen
- Two passengers wearing white hats
- A plane that doesn't fly
- A flying Ace
- A pen and paper
- Runners on a runway
- Five men blowing up a balloon
- Dracula
- Three childish pilots
- Eighteen airport workers with yellow caps

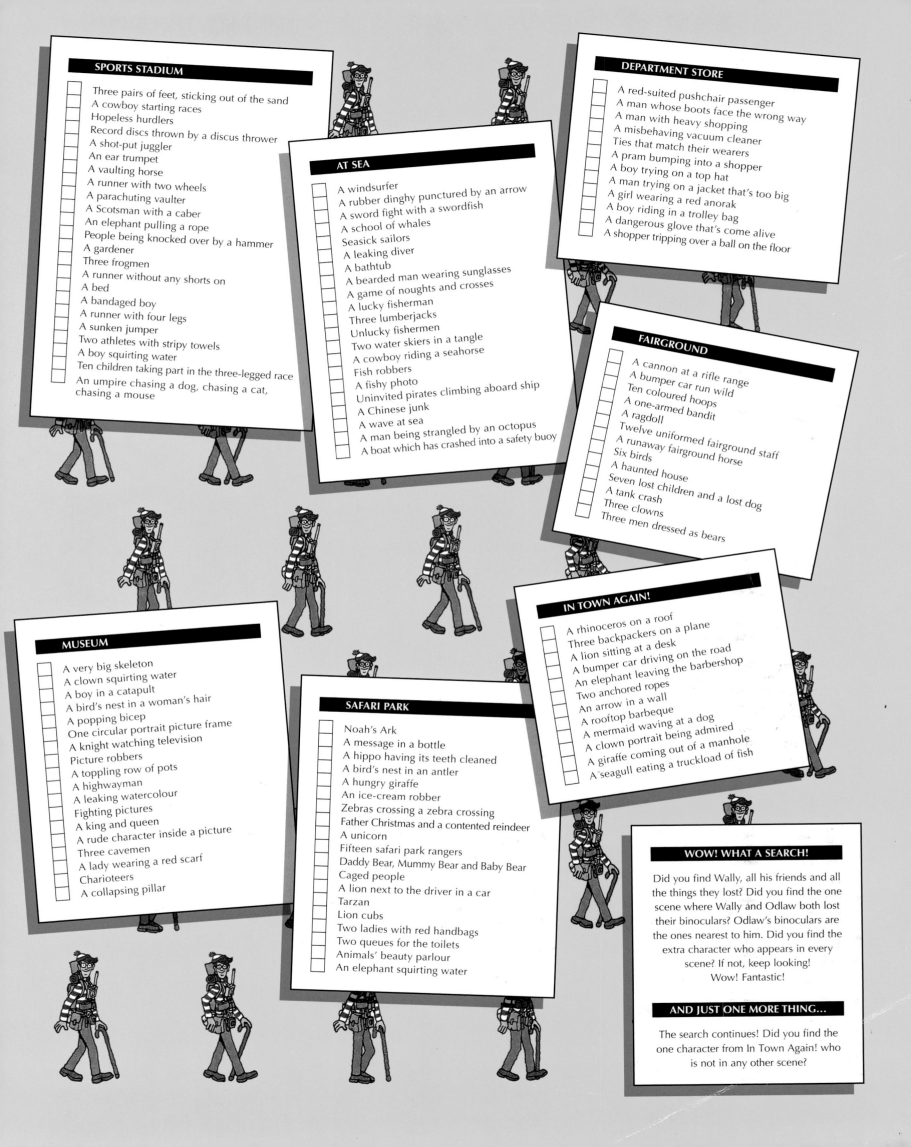

SPORTS STADIUM

- Three pairs of feet, sticking out of the sand
- A cowboy starting races
- Hopeless hurdlers
- Record discs thrown by a discus thrower
- A shot-put juggler
- An ear trumpet
- A vaulting horse
- A runner with two wheels
- A parachuting vaulter
- A Scotsman with a caber
- An elephant pulling a rope
- People being knocked over by a hammer
- A gardener
- Three frogmen
- A runner without any shorts on
- A bed
- A bandaged boy
- A runner with four legs
- A sunken jumper
- Two athletes with stripy towels
- A boy squirting water
- Ten children taking part in the three-legged race
- An umpire chasing a dog, chasing a cat, chasing a mouse

AT SEA

- A windsurfer
- A rubber dinghy punctured by an arrow
- A sword fight with a swordfish
- A school of whales
- Seasick sailors
- A leaking diver
- A bathtub
- A bearded man wearing sunglasses
- A game of noughts and crosses
- A lucky fisherman
- Three lumberjacks
- Unlucky fishermen
- Two water skiers in a tangle
- A cowboy riding a seahorse
- Fish robbers
- A fishy photo
- Uninvited pirates climbing aboard ship
- A Chinese junk
- A wave at sea
- A man being strangled by an octopus
- A boat which has crashed into a safety buoy

DEPARTMENT STORE

- A red-suited pushchair passenger
- A man whose boots face the wrong way
- A man with heavy shopping
- A misbehaving vacuum cleaner
- Ties that match their wearers
- A pram bumping into a shopper
- A boy trying on a top hat
- A man trying on a jacket that's too big
- A girl wearing a red anorak
- A boy riding in a trolley bag
- A dangerous glove that's come alive
- A shopper tripping over a ball on the floor

FAIRGROUND

- A cannon at a rifle range
- A bumper car run wild
- Ten coloured hoops
- A one-armed bandit
- A ragdoll
- Twelve uniformed fairground staff
- A runaway fairground horse
- Six birds
- A haunted house
- Seven lost children and a lost dog
- A tank crash
- Three clowns
- Three men dressed as bears

MUSEUM

- A very big skeleton
- A clown squirting water
- A boy in a catapult
- A bird's nest in a woman's hair
- A popping bicep
- One circular portrait picture frame
- A knight watching television
- Picture robbers
- A toppling row of pots
- A highwayman
- A leaking watercolour
- Fighting pictures
- A king and queen
- A rude character inside a picture
- Three cavemen
- A lady wearing a red scarf
- Charioteers
- A collapsing pillar

SAFARI PARK

- Noah's Ark
- A message in a bottle
- A hippo having its teeth cleaned
- A bird's nest in an antler
- A hungry giraffe
- An ice-cream robber
- Zebras crossing a zebra crossing
- Father Christmas and a contented reindeer
- A unicorn
- Fifteen safari park rangers
- Daddy Bear, Mummy Bear and Baby Bear
- Caged people
- A lion next to the driver in a car
- Tarzan
- Lion cubs
- Two ladies with red handbags
- Two queues for the toilets
- Animals' beauty parlour
- An elephant squirting water

IN TOWN AGAIN!

- A rhinoceros on a roof
- Three backpackers on a plane
- A lion sitting at a desk
- A bumper car driving on the road
- An elephant leaving the barbershop
- Two anchored ropes
- An arrow in a wall
- A rooftop barbeque
- A mermaid waving at a dog
- A clown portrait being admired
- A giraffe coming out of a manhole
- A seagull eating a truckload of fish

WOW! WHAT A SEARCH!

Did you find Wally, all his friends and all the things they lost? Did you find the one scene where Wally and Odlaw both lost their binoculars? Odlaw's binoculars are the ones nearest to him. Did you find the extra character who appears in every scene? If not, keep looking!
Wow! Fantastic!

AND JUST ONE MORE THING...

The search continues! Did you find the one character from In Town Again! who is not in any other scene?

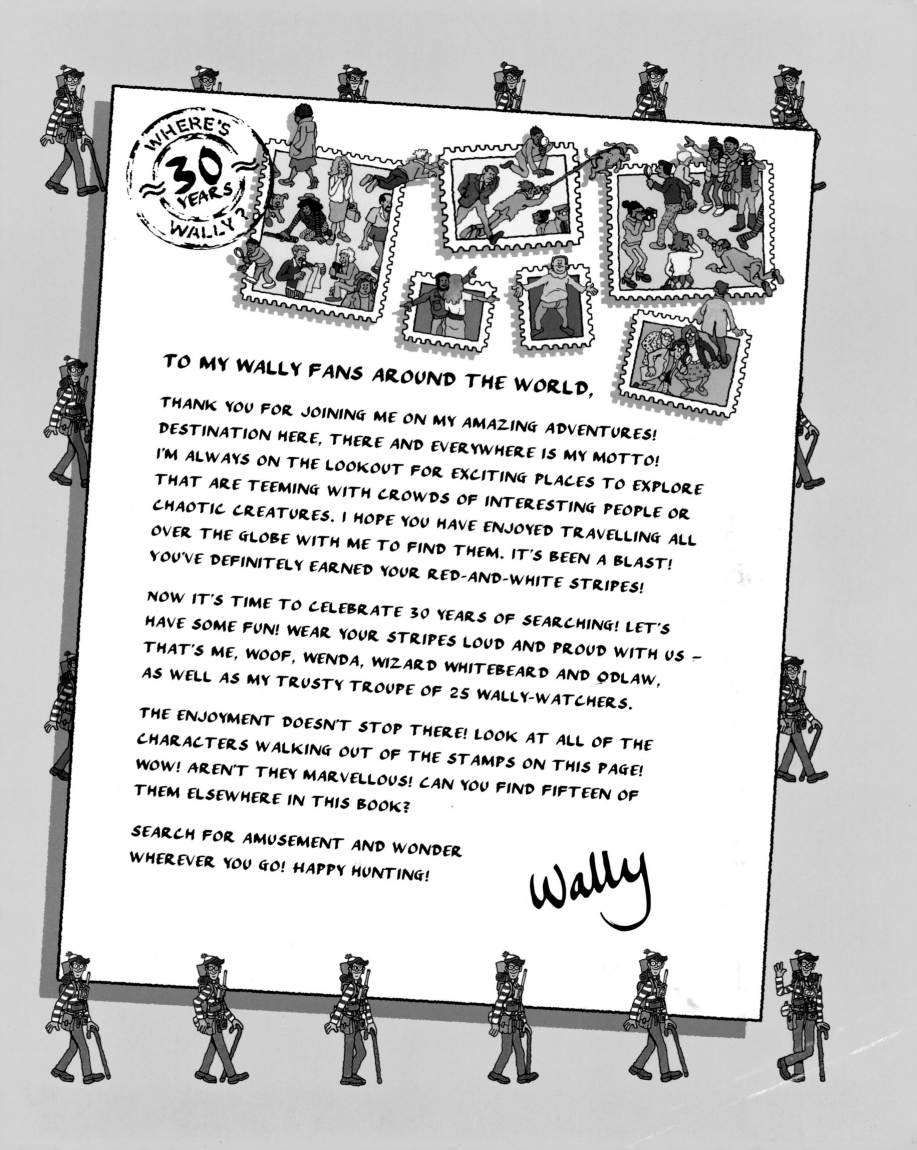

TO MY WALLY FANS AROUND THE WORLD,

THANK YOU FOR JOINING ME ON MY AMAZING ADVENTURES!
DESTINATION HERE, THERE AND EVERYWHERE IS MY MOTTO!
I'M ALWAYS ON THE LOOKOUT FOR EXCITING PLACES TO EXPLORE
THAT ARE TEEMING WITH CROWDS OF INTERESTING PEOPLE OR
CHAOTIC CREATURES. I HOPE YOU HAVE ENJOYED TRAVELLING ALL
OVER THE GLOBE WITH ME TO FIND THEM. IT'S BEEN A BLAST!
YOU'VE DEFINITELY EARNED YOUR RED-AND-WHITE STRIPES!

NOW IT'S TIME TO CELEBRATE 30 YEARS OF SEARCHING! LET'S
HAVE SOME FUN! WEAR YOUR STRIPES LOUD AND PROUD WITH US —
THAT'S ME, WOOF, WENDA, WIZARD WHITEBEARD AND ODLAW,
AS WELL AS MY TRUSTY TROUPE OF 25 WALLY-WATCHERS.

THE ENJOYMENT DOESN'T STOP THERE! LOOK AT ALL OF THE
CHARACTERS WALKING OUT OF THE STAMPS ON THIS PAGE!
WOW! AREN'T THEY MARVELLOUS! CAN YOU FIND FIFTEEN OF
THEM ELSEWHERE IN THIS BOOK?

SEARCH FOR AMUSEMENT AND WONDER
WHEREVER YOU GO! HAPPY HUNTING!

Wally